T H E
Ugly
Menorah

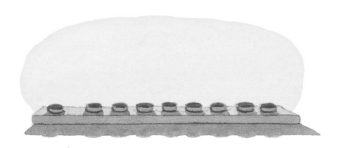

M A R I S S A   M O S S

A Sunburst Book • Farrar, Straus and Giroux

For Steven, who remembers Grandpa's hands

Copyright © 1996 by Marissa Moss

All rights reserved

Distributed in Canada by Douglas & McIntyre Ltd.

Color separations by Hong Kong Scanner Arts

Printed in the United States of America by Worzalla

Typography by Filomena Tuosto

First edition, 1996

Sunburst edition, 2000

10 9 8 7 6 5 4 3 2

Library of Congress Cataloging-in-Publication Data

Moss, Marissa.

 The ugly menorah / Marissa Moss.

  p. cm.

 Summary: For the first time since her grandfather's death, Rachel feels
close to him as she and her grandmother celebrate Hanukkah with the
simple menorah that he had made many years ago.

 ISBN: 0-374-48047-8 (pbk.)

 [1. Grandfathers—Fiction. 2. Hanukkah—Fiction.] I. Title.

PZ7.M8535Ug 1996

[E]—dc20   95-33260

Hanukkah commemorates an ancient struggle for religious freedom. When Antiochus became ruler of Judaea, he decreed that Jews could no longer practice their religion. Instead, they must honor the idols representing the Greek gods. Any who refused would be killed.

The soldiers ransacked the Temple, the Jewish house of worship, in Jerusalem. The oil lamp, which was always lit, was overturned; holy books were burned; the altar was desecrated. Led by Mattathias and his sons, the Maccabees, the Jews rebelled. Even though they were few and the soldiers were many, the Jews won. This was the first miracle of Hanukkah.

The Jews cleaned out the Temple and rededicated it. For eight days, they celebrated both their victory and the renewal of the Temple. According to later tradition, when the Jews tried to relight the lamp in the Temple, they found only enough oil for one day. But the flame lasted for eight days. This was considered the second miracle of Hanukkah.

To mark these eight days, a new candle is lit in the menorah on each night of the holiday, starting with one and ending with all eight on the final night. It is customary to eat foods fried in oil as a reminder of the miracle of the oil. In Israel, jelly doughnuts are eaten. In America and Europe, eating potato pancakes called latkes is the custom. Playing dreidl, a gambling game using a top with Hebrew letters on it, is also part of the celebration.

Although exchanging presents at Hanukkah the way Christians do at Christmas has become popular among Jews, many are now looking for ways to get back to the original holiday and its meaning, stressing religious freedom and the strength of faith. In these families, Hanukkah is not so much a time for giving gifts as a holiday for sharing and rejoicing in our freedom to live a Jewish life.

Rachel loved the heavy silver menorah her family used every Hanukkah. All year long, it sat in the cupboard, hidden from sight, but once a year, at Hanukkah, her father brought it down and polished it and set it in the window. It was beautiful and elegant, with vines etched into the branches, and a Star of David. Each night they added another candle, until the entire menorah looked magical in a gold and silver glow.

This Hanukkah was different. Since school was out, and it was the first Hanukkah after Rachel's grandpa had died, Rachel was staying with her grandma to keep her company. Rachel had loved visiting her grandparents. Their house used to be full of interesting things that Grandpa was working on. But without Grandpa the house felt colder, emptier. All the junk he had collected to make things with was gone. His work gloves weren't hanging on the hook in the kitchen anymore. Only his reading chair was left, and it seemed lonely and sad to Rachel. She sat in it and tried to feel Grandpa next to her, but she couldn't.

"Come into the kitchen," Grandma called. "I need your help grating potatoes for the latkes tonight."

"Yummy!" said Rachel. "I love latkes and applesauce."

"What would Hanukkah be without latkes?" Grandma said. "I know they're traditional, but to me latkes just taste good. They taste like Hanukkah."

"Where is your menorah, Grandma?" Rachel asked.

"It's right there," said Grandma. She pointed to a plain wooden board with tin cylinders to hold the candles. It was not at all like the elegant silver menorah at home.

"It's so ugly!" Rachel cried.

Grandma smiled. "I suppose it looks that way. But I love it because Grandpa made it for me. Do you want to hear the story?"

Rachel thought that Hanukkah would be ruined with such an ugly menorah, but she nodded.

"Well," said Grandma, "it was a long time ago,
when we first got married. Because of the Depression,
we didn't have much money. Hanukkah was coming,
and we had no menorah to light the candles in.

"Every day I passed the shop windows and looked at the different menorahs. I even picked out the one I wanted. Oh, it was beautiful! Shiny silver, with wonderful designs worked into it, grapes and leaves and lions, and a Star of David. It should belong to a queen, that menorah!

"Your grandpa knew I wanted that menorah. He tried so hard to get it for me. He worked long hours at the tailor shop, but he couldn't earn enough money for even the simplest menorah.

"But, walking home every day, Grandpa passed a construction site—a big building was going up. Scraps of wood were lying all around. Bits of tin gleamed in the dirt. Grandpa went up to the foreman and asked if he could have some of the leftover cuttings. The foreman laughed. 'It's junk, trash! Take all you want,' he said."

Rachel smiled. "So Grandpa was collecting junk even back then."

"Yes," said Grandma. "But it wasn't junk to him, not to Grandpa.

"Anyway," Grandma said, "it was the first night of Hanukkah. I made latkes and applesauce and waited for Grandpa. When he opened the door, he could smell how delicious everything was and he smiled a big smile. I was a little sad we had no menorah, but I smiled, too, and pretended it didn't matter.

"Then Grandpa handed me a package wrapped in newspaper. I couldn't think what it could be! I tore open the paper and there was this, our menorah. Grandpa had made it from those scraps of wood and tin. Oh, it certainly wasn't fit for a queen. But it was perfect for us.

"And I was so happy to be lighting the candles and saying the blessings over our own menorah that by the eighth night, when all the flames were dancing, I thought it was the most beautiful menorah in the world. And, you know, I still think so."

Rachel looked again at the plain little menorah. She remembered Grandpa's strong, knotty hands and the toys he had made with them for her, all from things he had found on the street: the rocking horse, the building blocks, the dollhouse.

"I miss Grandpa," Rachel said.

"Me, too." Grandma sighed.

But it still isn't beautiful, Rachel thought. "I'm sorry you couldn't have a real menorah," she said, "like the one you saw in the shop window."

"Oh," said Grandma, "it's real."

That night Grandma lit the first candle with the *shammes*, the candle that is used to light the others, and she and Rachel chanted the Hanukkah blessing together:

"Baruch atah adonai eloheinu melech ha'olam asher kid'shanu b'mitzvotav v'tzivanu l'hadlik ner shel hanukkah.

"Blessed art thou, O Lord, our God, ruler of the Universe, who has sanctified us with the Commandments and commanded us to kindle the Hanukkah lights."

Rachel watched the flames flickering yellow, then blue, then white. For the first time since Grandpa died, she felt he was with her again. She could hear his gravelly voice saying the prayer, she could smell his pepperminty and woolly smell, she could see his slow, gentle turtle smile in the glowing candlelight.

Rachel hugged Grandma. "I see why you love your menorah so much," she said.

On the last night of Hanukkah, Rachel's parents came to celebrate with them before taking Rachel home the next day.

"Oh, Mama," Rachel's mother said, "do you still have that old menorah? Why don't you buy a new one like ours?"

"I don't need a new one," Grandma said. "Do I, Rachel?"

"No," Rachel said. "This menorah is very special. And very beautiful."

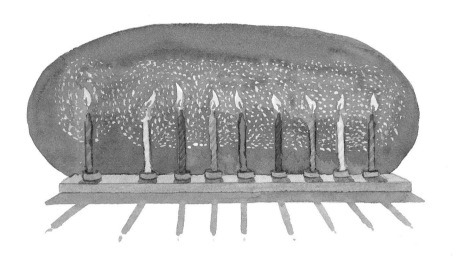